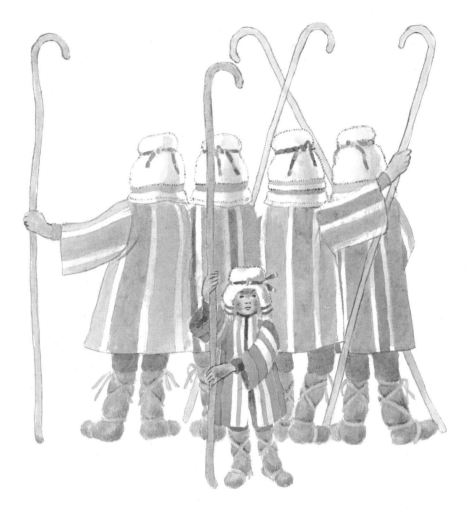

A CERTAIN SMALL SHEPHERD

A

BY REBECCA CAUDILL

Certain

WITH ILLUSTRATIONS BY WILLIAM PÈNE DU BOIS

Small Shepherd

HENRY HOLT AND COMPANY   NEW YORK

Henry Holt and Company, Inc.
Publishers since 1866
115 West 18th Street
New York, New York 10011

Henry Holt is a registered trademark of Henry Holt and Company, Inc.

Published in Canada by Fitzhenry & Whiteside Ltd.,
195 Allstate Parkway, Markham, Ontario L3R 4T8.
First published in hardcover in 1965 by
Henry Holt and Company, Inc.
First paperback edition, 1997

Library of Congress Catalog Number: 65-17604

ISBN 0-8050-1323-7 (hardcover)
10 12 14 16 18 20 19 17 15 13 11

ISBN 0-8050-5392-1 (paperback)
1 3 5 7 9 10 8 6 4 2
Printed in Mexico.

In loving memory of
Jimmy,
who, one Christmas, was
a small and listening shepherd.

This is a story of a strange and a marvelous thing. It happened on a Christmas morning at Hurricane Gap, and not so long ago at that.

But before you hear about Christmas morning, you must hear about Christmas Eve, for that is part of the story.

And before you hear about Christmas Eve, you must hear about Jamie, for without Jamie there would be no story.

Jamie was born on a freakish night in November. The cold that night moved down from the North and rested its heavy hand suddenly on Hurricane Gap. Within an hour's time, the naked earth turned brittle. Line Fork Creek froze solid in its winding bed and lay motionless, like a string dropped at the foot of Pine Mountain.

Nothing but the dark wind was abroad in the hollow.

7

Wild creatures huddled in their dens. Cows stood hunched in their stalls. Housewives stuffed rags in the cracks underneath their doors against the needling cold, and men heaped oak and apple wood on their fires.

At the foot of the Gap, where Jamie's house stood, the wind doubled its fury. It battered the doors of the house. It rattled the windows. It wailed like a banshee in the chimney.

"For sure, it's bad luck trying to break in," moaned Jamie's mother, and turned her face to her pillow.

"Bad luck has no business here," Jamie's father said bravely.

He laid more logs on the fire. Flames licked at them and roared up the chimney. But through the roaring, the wind wailed on, thin and high.

Father took the newborn baby from the bed beside its mother and sat holding it on his knee.

"Saro," he called, "you and Honey come see Jamie!"

Two girls came from the shadows of the room. In the firelight they stood looking at the tiny wrinkled red face inside the blanket.

"He's such a little brother!" said Saro.

8

"Give him time. He'll grow," said Father proudly. "When he's three, he'll be as big as Honey. When he's six, he'll be as big as you. You want to hold him?"

Saro sat down on a stool and Father laid the bundle in her arms.

Honey stood beside Saro. She pulled back a corner of the blanket. She opened one of the tiny hands and laid one of her fingers in it. She smiled at the face in the blanket. She looked up, smiling, at Father.

But Father did not see her. He was standing beside Mother, trying to comfort her.

That night Jamie's mother died.

Jamie ate and slept and grew.

Like other babies, he cut teeth. He learned to sit alone and to crawl. When he was a year old, he toddled about like other one-year-olds. At two, he carried around sticks and stones like other two-year-olds. He threw balls and built towers of blocks and knocked them down.

Everything that other two-year-olds could do, Jamie could do, except one thing. He could not talk.

The old women of Hurricane Gap sat in their chimney corners and shook their heads.

"His mother, poor soul, should have rubbed him with lard," said one.

"She ought to have brushed him with a rabbit's foot," said another.

"Wasn't that boy born on a Wednesday?" asked another. " 'Wednesday's child is full of woe,' " she quoted from an old saying.

"Jamie gets everything he wants by pointing," explained Father. "Give him time. He'll learn to talk."

At three, Jamie could zip his shirt and tie his shoes.

At four, he followed Father to the stable at milking time. He milked the kittens' pan full of milk.

But even at four, Jamie could not talk like other children. He could only make strange grunting noises.

One day Jamie found a litter of new kittens in a box under the stairs. He ran to the cornfield to tell Father. He wanted to say he had been feeling around in the box for a ball he'd lost, and suddenly his fingers had felt something warm and squirmy, and here were all these kittens.

But how could you tell somebody something if, when you opened your mouth, you could only grunt?

Jamie started running. He ran till he reached the orchard. There, he threw himself face down in the tall grass and kicked his feet against the ground.

13

One day Honey's friends came to play hide-and-seek. Jamie played with them.

Because Clive was the oldest, he shut his eyes first and counted to fifty, while the other children scattered and hid behind trees in the yard and corners of the house. After he had counted to fifty, the hollow rang with cries.

"One, two, three for Milly!"

"One, two, three for Jamie!"

"One, two, three, I'm home free."

It came Jamie's turn to shut his eyes. He sat on the porch step, covered his eyes with his hands, and began to count.

"Listen to Jamie!" Clive called to the other children.

The others listened. Then they all began to laugh.

Jamie got up. He ran after the children. He fought them with both fists and both feet. Honey helped him.

Then Jamie ran away to the orchard, and threw himself down on his face in the tall grass, and kicked the ground.

Later, when Father was walking through the orchard, he came across Jamie lying in the grass.

"Jamie," said Father, "there's a new calf in the pasture. I need you to help me bring it to the stable."

Jamie got up from the grass. He wiped his eyes. Out of the orchard and across the pasture he trudged at Father's heels. In a far corner of the pasture they found the cow. Beside her, on wobbly legs, stood the new calf.

Together, Father and Jamie drove the cow and the calf to the stable, into an empty stall.

Together, they brought nubbins from the corncrib to feed the cow.

Together, they made a bed of clean hay for the calf.

"Jamie," said Father the next morning, "I need you to help plow the corn."

Father harnessed the horse and lifted Jamie to the horse's back. Away to the cornfield they went, Father walking in front of the horse, Jamie riding, holding tight to the hames.

While Father plowed, Jamie walked in the furrow behind him. When Father lay on his back in the shade of the persimmon tree to rest, Jamie lay beside him. Father told Jamie the names of the birds flying overhead—the turkey vulture tilting its uplifted wings against the white clouds, the carrion crow flapping lazily and sailing, flapping and

sailing, and the sharp-shinned hawk gliding to rest in the woodland.

The next day Jamie helped Father set out sweet potatoes. Other days he helped Father trim fence rows and mend fences.

Whatever Father did, Jamie helped him.

One day Father drove the car out of the shed and stopped in front of the house.

"Jamie!" he called. "Jump in. We're going across Pine Mountain."

"Can I go, too?" asked Honey.

"Not today," said Father. "I'm taking Jamie to see a doctor."

The doctor looked at Jamie's throat. He listened to Jamie grunt. He shook his head.

"You might see Dr. Jones," he said.

Father and Jamie got into the car and drove across Big Black Mountain to see Dr. Jones.

"Maybe Jamie could learn to talk," Dr. Jones said. "But he would have to be sent away to a special school. He would have to stay there several months. He might have to stay two or three years. Or four.

"It is a long time," said Dr. Jones.

"And the pocket is empty," said Father.

So Father and Jamie got into the car and started home.

Usually Father talked to Jamie as they drove along. Now they drove all the way, across Big Black and across Pine, without a word.

In August every year, school opened at Hurricane Gap.

On the first morning of school the year that Jamie was six, Father handed him a book, a tablet, a pencil, and a box of crayons—all shiny and new.

"You're going to school, Jamie," he said. "I'll go with you this morning."

The neighbors watched them walking down the road together, toward the little one-room schoolhouse.

"Poor foolish father!" they said, and shook their heads. "Trying to make somebody out of that no-account boy!"

Miss Creech, the teacher, shook her head too. With so many children, so many classes, so many grades, she hadn't time for a boy who couldn't talk, she told Father.

"What will Jamie do all day long?" she asked.

"He will listen," said Father.

So Jamie took his book and his tablet, his pencil and

his box of crayons, and sat down in an empty seat in the front row.

Every day Jamie listened. He learned the words on the pages of his book. He learned how to count. He liked the reading and the counting.

But the part of school Jamie liked best was the big piece of paper Miss Creech gave him every day. On it he printed words in squares, like the other children. He wrote numbers. He drew pictures and colored them with his crayons. He could say things on paper.

One day Miss Creech said Jamie had the best paper in the first grade. She held it up for all the children to see.

On sunny days on the playground the children played ball games and three-deep and duck-on-a-rock—games a boy can play without talking. On rainy days they played indoors.

One rainy day the children played a guessing game. Jamie knew the answer that no other child could guess. But he couldn't say the answer. He didn't know how to spell the answer. He could find nothing to point to that showed he knew the answer.

That evening at home he threw his book into a corner.

He slammed the door. He pulled Honey's hair. He twisted the cat's tail. The cat yowled and leaped under the bed.

"Jamie," said Father, "cats have feelings, just like boys."

Every year the people of Hurricane Gap celebrated Christmas in the little white church that stood across the road from Jamie's house. On Christmas Eve the boys and girls gave a Christmas play. People came miles to see it—from the other side of Pine Mountain and from the head of every creek and hollow. Miss Creech directed the play.

Through the late fall, as the leaves fell from the trees and the days grew shorter and the air snapped with cold, Jamie wondered when Miss Creech would talk about the play. Finally, one afternoon in November, Miss Creech announced it was time to begin play practice.

Jamie laid his book inside his desk and listened carefully as Miss Creech assigned the parts of the play.

Miss Creech gave the part of Mary to Joan, who lived up Pine Mountain beyond the rock quarry. She asked Honey to bring her big doll to be the Baby. She gave the part of Joseph to Henry, who lived at the head of Little Laurelpatch. She asked Saro to be an angel; Clive the innkeeper. She chose three big boys to be Wise Men, four others to be shepherds. She named the boys and girls who were to be people living in Bethlehem. The rest of the boys and girls would sing carols, she said.

Jamie for a moment listened to the sound of the words he had last heard. Yes, Miss Creech expected him to sing carols.

Every day after school the boys and girls went with Miss Creech up the road to the church and practiced the Christmas play.

Every day Jamie stood in the front row of the carolers. The first day he stood quietly. The second day he shoved Milly, who was standing next to him. The third day he pulled Honey's hair. The fourth day, when the carolers began singing, Jamie ran to the window, grabbed a ball from the sill, and bounced it across the floor.

"Wait a minute, children," Miss Creech said to the carolers.

She turned to Jamie.

"Jamie," she asked, "how would you like to be a shepherd?"

"He's too little," said one of the big shepherds.

"No, he isn't," said Saro. "If my father was a shepherd, Jamie would help him."

That afternoon Jamie became a small shepherd. He ran home after practice to tell Father.

Father couldn't understand what Jamie was telling him. But he knew that Jamie had been changed into somebody important.

One afternoon, at play practice, Miss Creech said to the boys and girls, "Forget you are Joan, and Henry, and Saro, and Clive, and Jamie. Remember that you are

Mary, and Joseph, and an angel, and an innkeeper, and a shepherd, and that strange things are happening in the hollow where you live.''

That night, at bedtime, Father took the big Bible off the table. Saro and Honey and Jamie gathered around the fire.

Over the room a hush fell as Father read:

And there were in the same country shepherds abiding in the field, keeping watch over their flock by night. And, lo, the angel of the Lord came upon them, and the glory of the Lord shone round about them: and they were sore afraid. And the angel said unto them, Fear not: for, behold, I bring you good tidings of great joy which shall be to all the people. . . . And it came to pass, as the angels were gone away from them into heaven, the shepherds said one to another, Let us now go even unto Bethlehem, and see this thing which is come to pass, which the Lord hath made known unto us. And they came with haste, and found Mary, and Joseph, and the babe lying in a manger.

Christmas drew near. At home in the evenings, when they had finished studying their lessons, the boys and girls of Hurricane Gap made decorations for the Christmas tree that would stand in the church. They glued together strips of bright-colored paper in long chains. They whittled stars and baby lambs and camels out of wild cherry wood. They strung long strings of popcorn.

Jamie strung a string of popcorn. Every night, as Father read from the Bible, Jamie added more kernels to his string.

"Jamie, are you trying to make a string long enough to reach to the top of Pine Mountain?" asked Honey one night.

Jamie did not hear her. He was far away, on a hillside, tending sheep. And even though he was a small shepherd and could only grunt when he tried to talk, an angel wrapped around with dazzling light was singling him out to tell him a wonderful thing that had happened down in the hollow in a cow stall.

He fell asleep, stringing his popcorn, and listening.

In a corner of the room where the fire burned, Father pulled from under his bed the trundle bed in which

Jamie slept. He turned back the covers, picked Jamie up from the floor, and laid him gently in the bed.

The next day Father went across Pine Mountain to the store. When he came home, he handed Saro a package. In it was cloth of four colors—green, gold, white, and red.

"Make Jamie a shepherd's coat, like the picture in the Bible," Father said to Saro.

Father went into the woods and found a crooked limb of a tree. He made it into a shepherd's crook for Jamie.

Jamie went to school the next morning carrying his shepherd's crook and his shepherd's coat on his arm. He would wear his coat and carry his crook when the boys and girls practiced the play.

All day Jamie waited patiently to practice the play. All day he sat listening.

But who could tell whose voice he heard? It might have been Miss Creech's. It might have been an angel's.

Two days before Christmas, Jamie's father and Clive's father drove in a pick-up truck along the Trace Branch road looking for a Christmas tree. On the mountainside they spotted a juniper growing broad and tall and free.

With axes they cut it down. They snaked it down the mountainside and loaded it into the truck.

Father had to open the doors of the church wide to get the tree inside. It reached to the ceiling. Frost-blue berries shone on its feathery green branches. The air around it smelled of spice.

That afternoon the mothers of Hurricane Gap, and Miss Creech, and all the boys and girls gathered at the church to decorate the tree.

In the tiptop of the tree they fastened the biggest star. Among the branches they hung the other stars and the baby lambs and camels whittled out of wild cherry wood. They hung polished red apples on twigs of the tree. They looped paper chains from branch to branch. Last of all, they festooned the tree with strings of snowy popcorn.

"Ah!" they said, as they looked at the tree. "Ah!"

Beside the tree the boys and girls practiced the Christmas play for the last time. When they had finished, they started home. Midway down the aisle they turned and looked again at the tree.

"Ah!" they said.

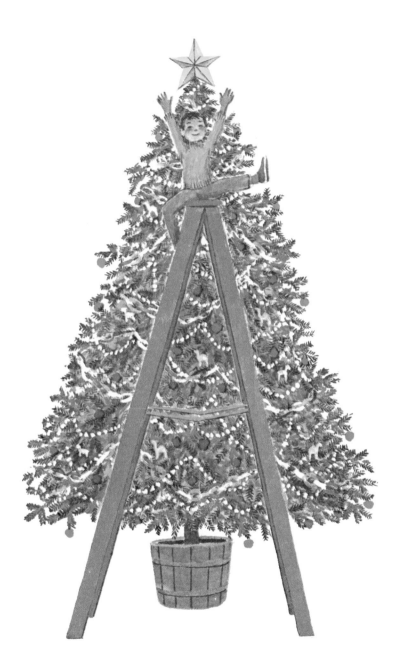

Saro opened the door. "Look!" she called. "Look, everybody! It's snowing!"

Jamie, the next morning, looked out on a world such as he had never seen. Hidden were the roads and the fences, the woodpile, and the swing under the oak tree—all buried deep under a lumpy quilt of snow. And before a stinging wind, snowflakes still madly whirled and danced.

Saro and Honey joined Jamie at the window.

"You can't see across Line Fork Creek in this storm," said Saro. "And where is Pine Mountain?"

"Where is the church?" asked Honey. "That's what I'd like to know."

Jamie turned to them with questions in his eyes.

"If it had been snowing hard that night in Bethlehem, Jamie," Honey told him, "the shepherds wouldn't have had their sheep out in the pasture. They would have had them in the stable, keeping them warm. Wouldn't they, Father? Then they wouldn't have heard what the angel said, all shut indoors like that."

"When angels have something to tell a shepherd," said Father, "they can find him in any place, in any sort of weather. If the shepherd is listening, he will hear."

At eleven o'clock the telephone rang.

"Hello!" said Father.

Saro and Honey and Jamie heard Miss Creech's voice. "I've just got the latest weather report. This storm is going on all day, and into the night. Do you think—"

The telephone, once it started ringing, wouldn't stop. No matter if it rang a long and a short, two longs and a short, a short and two longs, or whatever, everyone on the Hurricane Gap line listened. The news they heard was always bad. Drifts ten feet high were piled up along the Trace Branch road. . . . The boys and girls on Little Laurelpatch couldn't get out. Joseph lived on Little Laurelpatch. . . . The road up Pine Mountain through Hurricane Gap was closed, all the way to the rock quarry. Mary couldn't get down the mountain. . . . And then the telephone went silent, dead in the storm.

Meanwhile, the snow kept up its crazy dance before the wind. It drifted in great white mounds across the roads and in the fence rows.

"Nobody but a foolish man would take to the road on a day like this," said Father.

At dinner Jamie sat at the table staring at his plate.

"Shepherds must eat, Jamie," said Father.

"Honey and I don't feel like eating either, Jamie," said Saro. "But see how Honey is eating!"

Still Jamie stared at his plate.

"Know what?" asked Saro. "Because we're all disappointed, we won't save the Christmas stack cake for tomorrow. We'll have a slice today. As soon as you eat your dinner, Jamie."

Still Jamie stared at his plate. He did not touch his food.

"You think that play was real, don't you, Jamie?" said Honey. "It wasn't real. It was just a play we were giving, like some story we'd made up."

Jamie could hold his sobs no longer. His body heaved as he ran to Father.

Father laid an arm about Jamie's shoulders.

"Sometimes, Jamie," he said, "angels say to shepherds, 'Be of good courage.' "

On through the short afternoon the storm raged.

Father heaped more wood on the fire. Saro sat in front of the fire reading a book. Honey cracked hickory nuts on the stone hearth. Jamie sat.

"Bring the popper, Jamie, and I'll pop some corn for you," said Father.

Jamie shook his head.

"Want me to read to you?" asked Saro.

Jamie shook his head.

"Why don't you help Honey crack hickory nuts?" asked Father.

Jamie shook his head.

"Jamie still thinks he's a shepherd," said Honey.

After a while Jamie left the fire and stood at the window, watching the wild storm. He squinted his eyes and stared. He motioned to Father to come and look. Saro and Honey, too, hurried to the window and looked.

Through the snowdrifts trudged a man, followed by a woman. They were bundled and buttoned from head to foot, and their faces were lowered against the wind and the flying snowflakes.

"Lord have mercy!" said Father, as he watched them turn in at the gate.

Around the house the man and the woman made their way to the back door. As Father opened the door to them, a gust of snow-laden wind whisked into the kitchen.

35

"Come in out of the cold," said Father.

The man and the woman stepped inside. They stamped their feet on the kitchen floor and brushed the snow from their clothes. They followed Father into the front room and sat down before the fire in the chairs Father told Saro to bring for them. Father, too, sat down.

Jamie stood beside Father. Saro and Honey stood be-

"It's cold in that stable," he said, as he started out the kitchen door. "Bitter cold."

On the doorstep he turned. "Don't wait up for me," he called back. "I may be gone a good while."

Over the earth darkness thickened. Still the wind blew and the snow whirled.

The clock on the mantel struck seven.

"I wish Father would come!" said Honey.

The clock struck eight. It ticked solemnly in the quiet house, where Saro and Honey and Jamie waited.

"Why doesn't Father come?" complained Honey.

"Why don't you hang up your stocking and go to bed?" asked Saro. "Jamie, it's time to hang up your stocking, too, and go to bed."

Jamie did not answer. He sat staring into the fire.

"That Jamie! He still thinks he's a shepherd!" said Honey, as she hung her stocking under the mantel.

"Jamie," said Saro, "aren't you going to hang up your stocking and go to bed?" She pulled the trundle bed from beneath Father's bed, and turned back the covers. She turned back the covers on Father's bed. She hung up her stocking and followed Honey upstairs.

"Jamie!" she called back.

Still Jamie stared into the fire. A strange feeling was growing inside him. This night was not like other nights, he knew. Something mysterious was going on. He felt afraid.

What was that he heard? The wind? Only the wind?

He lay down on his bed with his clothes on. He dropped off to sleep. A rattling at the door waked him.

He sat upright quickly. He looked around. His heart beat fast. But nothing in the room had changed. Everything was as it had been when he lay down—the fire was burning; two stockings, Saro's and Honey's, hung under the mantel; the clock was ticking solemnly.

He looked at Father's bed. The sheets were just as Saro had turned them back.

There! There it was! He heard it again! It sounded like singing. "Glory to God! On earth peace!"

Jamie breathed hard. Had he heard that? Or had he only said it to himself?

He lay down again and pulled the quilts over his head.

"Get up, Jamie," he heard Father saying. "Put your clothes on, quick."

Jamie opened his eyes. He saw daylight seeping into the room. He saw Father standing over him, bundled in warm clothes.

Wondering, Jamie flung the quilts back and rolled out of bed.

"Why, Jamie," said Father, "you're already dressed!"

Father went to the stairs. "Saro! Honey!" he called. "Come quick!"

"What's happened, Father?" asked Saro.

"What are we going to do?" asked Honey, as she fumbled sleepily with her shoe laces.

"Come with me," said Father.

"Where are we going?" asked Honey.

"To the stable?" asked Saro.

"The stable was no fit place," said Father. "Not on this bitter night. Not when the church was close by, and it with a stove in it and coal for burning."

Out into the cold, silent, white morning they went. The wind had laid. Snow no longer fell. The clouds were lifting. One star in the vast sky, its brilliance fading in the growing light, shone down on Hurricane Gap.

Father led the way through the drifted snow. The

others followed, stepping in his tracks.

As Father pushed open the church door, the fragrance of the Christmas tree rushed out at them. The potbellied stove glowed red with the fire within.

Muffling his footsteps, Father walked quietly up the

aisle. Wonderingly, the others followed. There, beside the star-crowned Christmas tree, where the Christmas play was to have been given, they saw the woman. She lay on the old buffalo skin, covered with quilts. Beside her pallet sat the man.

The woman smiled at them. "You came to see?" she asked, and lifted the cover.

Saro went first and peeped under the cover. Honey went next.

"You look too, Jamie," said Saro.

For a second Jamie hesitated. He leaned forward and took one quick look. Then he turned, shot down the aisle and out of the church, slamming the door behind him.

Saro ran down the church aisle, calling after him.

"Wait, Saro," said Father, watching Jamie through the window.

To the house Jamie made his way, half running along the path Father's big boots had cut through the snow-drifts.

Inside the house he hurriedly pulled his shepherd's robe over his coat. He snatched up his crook from the chimney corner.

With his hand on the doorknob, he glanced toward the fireplace. There, under the mantel, hung Saro's and Honey's stockings. And there, beside them, hung his stocking! Now who had hung it there? It had in it the same bulge his stocking had had every Christmas morning since he could remember—a bulge made by an orange.

Jamie ran to the fireplace and felt the toe of his stocking. Yes, there was the dime, just as on other Christmas mornings.

Hurriedly he emptied his stocking. With the orange and the dime in one hand and the crook in the other, he made his way toward the church. Father and Saro, still watching, saw his shepherd's robe a spot of glowing color in a great white world.

Father opened the church door.

Without looking to left or right, Jamie hurried up the aisle. Father and Saro followed him. Beside the pallet he dropped to his knees.

"Here's a Christmas gift for the Child," he said, clear and strong.

"Father!" gasped Saro. "Father, listen to Jamie!"

The woman turned back the covers from the baby's face. Jamie gently laid the orange beside the baby's tiny hand.

"And here's a Christmas gift for the Mother," Jamie said to the woman.

He put the dime in her hand.

Father, trembling with wonder and with joy, fell to his knees beside Jamie. Saro, too, knelt; and Honey, and the man.

"Surely," the woman spoke softly, "the Lord lives this day."

"Surely," said Father, "the Lord does live this day, and all days. And he is loving and merciful and good."

In the hush that followed, Christmas in all its joy and majesty came to Hurricane Gap. And it wasn't so long ago at that.